Roxie
the Baking
Fairy

Special thanks to Narinder Dhami

No part of this publication may be reproduced, stored in a
retrieval system, or transmitted in any form or by any means,
electronic, mechanical, photocopying, recording, or otherwise,
without written permission of the publisher. For information
regarding permission, write to Rainbow Magic Limited,
c/o HIT Entertainment, 830 South Greenville Avenue, Allen, TX
75002-3320.

ISBN 978-0-545-70835-7

All rights reserved. Published by Scholastic Inc., 557 Broadway,
New York, NY 10012, by arrangement with Rainbow Magic
Limited.

12 11 10 9 8 7 6 5 4 3 2 1   15 16 17 18 19 20/0

Printed in the U.S.A.   40

This edition first printing, March 2015

Roxie
the Baking
Fairy

by Daisy Meadows

SCHOLASTIC INC.

The Fairyland Palace

Sara Sketchley's house

Bridge

Maze

Rainspell Island

Park

Carrie's Jewelry Shop

Beach and Boardwalk

Jack Frost's
Ice Castle

Campsite

Walkers'
tent

Daffodil
cottage

Market Square

Pottery Hall

Sunshine
Cake Shop

Polly Painterly's Workshop

I'm a wonderful painter—have you heard of me?
Behold my artistic ability!
With palette, brush, and paints in hand,
I'll be the most famous artist in all the land!

The Magical Crafts Fairies can't stop me!
I'll steal their magic, and then you'll see
That everyone, no matter what the cost,
Will want a painting done by Jack Frost!

Contents

Exhibition Day

"I'm so sad that it's our last day of vacation." Kirsty Tate sighed, placing a pile of folded T-shirts in her suitcase. "But I'm super excited about the Crafts Week exhibition and competition today!"

"So am I," Rachel Walker agreed. The girls were in Kirsty's attic bedroom at the b and b, getting their things ready to head home that evening. They'd spent the week on Rainspell Island, staying every other night at the b and b with Mr. and Mrs. Tate, and alternate nights at the campsite with Rachel's parents.

"It's been so much fun trying out all these different crafts, hasn't it?" said Kirsty enthusiastically, and Rachel nodded. It was Crafts Week on Rainspell Island, and for the past six days the girls had attended all sorts of workshops. Today there was an exhibition of the best crafts created during the week. Prizes were going to be awarded!

"And isn't it great that we *both* have entries in the exhibition, Kirsty?" Rachel asked, stuffing socks into her suitcase. "I think your painting of me under a rainbow should definitely win a prize."

"No, I think your story about us meeting the Rainbow Fairies on our first visit to Rainspell Island should win!" Kirsty laughed. "Of course, no one except us knows that it's all true!"

At that moment, Mrs. Tate came in. "Girls, have you finished packing yet?" she asked.

"Almost, Mom," Kirsty replied, putting her bathroom bag into her suitcase. "Can we bring our entries to Artie for the exhibition now?" Artie Johnson was the organizer of the Rainspell Island Crafts Week.

"Then we agreed to help bake cakes and cookies to serve at the exhibition this afternoon," Rachel added.

"I'm looking forward to tasting them!" Mrs. Tate said with a smile. "Off you go! We'll see you at the exhibition later."

The girls called good-bye to Mr. Tate and hurried out of the b and b. Rachel carried the notebook that author Poppy Fields had given her at the writing workshop, and Kirsty had her painting tucked under her arm.

A huge tent had been set up on the boardwalk for the exhibition. The girls slipped inside and quickly found Artie and her helpers setting up tables.

"Hello, girls," Artie said, beaming at them. "Do you have something for me?"

Rachel and Kirsty handed over the

notebook and painting.

"Good luck in the competition," Artie told them. "What are you doing until then?"

"We're going to the Sunshine  Cake Shop," Rachel explained. "We're helping bake goodies for the exhibition."

"My husband, Ben, is the head baker there," Artie said, her eyes twinkling. "I'm sure he'll be delighted to have some extra hands helping out!"

After saying good-bye to Artie, the girls left the tent and walked back along the boardwalk to Main Street.

"The exhibition is going to be so much fun!" Rachel said excitedly. "As long as Jack Frost doesn't ruin everything," Kirsty replied with a sigh. Jack Frost had been up to his old tricks again!

When Rachel and Kirsty arrived on Rainspell Island, they'd been invited to Fairyland by Kayla the Pottery Fairy, one of the seven Magical Crafts Fairies. The girls had been excited to discover that not only was it Crafts Week on Rainspell Island, it was Magical Crafts Week in Fairyland, too! Kayla had explained that King Oberon and Queen Titania would choose the most impressive fairy crafts to decorate their royal palace.

But before Magical Crafts Week could get underway, Jack Frost and his goblins had shown up, throwing paint-filled balloons into the crowd. Green paint had splattered everywhere! In the confusion, Jack Frost had snatched the Magical Crafts Fairies' special objects. Determined to be the best artist ever, Jack Frost had used his icy magic to whisk himself, his goblins, and the magic objects away to the human world. Rachel and Kirsty knew that it was the Magical Crafts Fairies' job to make sure that humans and fairies had fun doing arts and crafts. But without their magic objects, the fairies were almost powerless! So Rachel and Kirsty had set out to find all the magic objects, with the fairies' help.

"We can't let Jack Frost ruin the last day of Crafts Week. We just can't!" Rachel said firmly.

"There's only one magic object left to find," Kirsty reminded her. She began to count them. "Kayla the Pottery Fairy, Annabelle the Drawing Fairy, Zadie the Sewing Fairy, Josie the Jewelry Fairy, Violet the Painting Fairy, Libby the Writing Fairy . . ." Then Kirsty gasped. Uh-oh!

"Rachel!" she cried. "The last missing object must belong to Roxie the *Baking* Fairy!"

"Oh, no!" Rachel groaned. "That means everything we bake for the exhibition will be terrible — unless we can find Roxie's magic object before this afternoon!"

The Great Bake-Off Disaster!

A little while later, the girls arrived at the Sunshine Cake Shop on the other end of Main Street. The windows of the bakery were filled with trays of cream cakes, fruit tarts, pretty pastel-colored cupcakes, and chocolate brownies. Their mouths watering, Rachel and Kirsty went inside.

"Hello, girls! Are you here to help with the baking for the exhibition?" a man in a white apron asked, poking his head out of a door at the back of the shop.

"Yes, we are," Kirsty replied.

"Come and join us in the kitchen," the man said, smiling. "I'm Ben Johnson, Artie's husband."

The girls hurried into the kitchen. They were happy to see some of the other kids who'd been at the workshops with them all week, plus some of the instructors, including author Poppy Fields, Polly Painterly the artist, Clayton Potts the potter, and jeweler Carrie Silver.

Ben had already laid out flour, sugar, eggs, and other ingredients on the counter, along with bowls, wooden spoons, measuring cups, and electric mixers. He handed out aprons, chefs' hats, and different recipe cards. Rachel got lemon drizzle cake, and Kirsty got sugar cookies.

"Okay, everyone, as you know, we want some wonderful cakes and cookies for the Crafts Week finale this afternoon!" Ben said.

Everyone began gathering their ingredients. Rachel picked up an egg carton, but it slipped from her hands. All the eggs smashed on the floor!

"What a klutz I am!" Rachel groaned.

"Don't worry," Ben said. "We have plenty more." But as he brought some fresh eggs over to Rachel, there was a cry from Polly Painterly, who was making a banana chocolate chip cake.

"Look out for that banana peel on the floor!" she exclaimed.

She was too late! Ben slipped on the
banana peel and knocked Carrie Silver's
bowl of coffee-and-walnut cake batter
onto the floor. Then one of the kids
dropped a bag of powdered sugar. The
box hit the floor, and the powdered sugar
billowed out in a big white cloud.
Everyone started coughing!

"Oh, no!" Kirsty suddenly cried in surprise. "I should have put a teaspoon of salt and a cup of sugar in my cookie dough—but I switched them around! I'll have to throw this salty batter away."

"This is all because Roxie the Baking Fairy doesn't have her magic object!" Rachel whispered.

Ben helped Carrie clean up her mess, and they started the cake again. But when Ben switched on the electric mixer to beat the butter and sugar with the flour and eggs, he gave a yelp as the mixture flew *everywhere*! People ducked as it splattered the counters, the windows, and even the ceiling.

"This kitchen is a disaster zone!" Rachel said, wiping a splotch of cake mix off her nose. She picked up her mixing bowl—and, to her amazement, out fluttered Roxie the Baking Fairy, shaking powdered sugar from her wings!

Star Shapes

"Hello, girls," Roxie murmured. She looked very pretty in her pink, full-skirted dress with a ruffled petticoat peeking out. On her feet were pink ballet flats decorated with tiny gold stars. "I'm sure you've been expecting me. This kitchen is a mess!"

"You can say that again, Roxie!" Rachel whispered as a burning smell filled the air.

"My peanut butter cookies!" one of the kids yelled. Ben dashed over to an oven and pulled open the door. Smoke poured out as he removed a tray of burned cookies. Everyone gathered around to look.

"Girls, will you help me get my magic star-shaped cookie cutter back?" Roxie asked while everyone else was distracted.

"Those goblins must be around here somewhere."

"Of course we will," Kirsty replied.

Flashing the girls a grateful smile, Roxie dove inside Kirsty's apron pocket.

"We have to find that cookie cutter, and *fast*," Rachel told Kirsty. "Otherwise, there will be no cakes or cookies at all for the exhibition this afternoon."

"Well, this looks wonderful!" Ben said suddenly from the other side of the kitchen.

Curious, Rachel and Kirsty turned to see what he was talking about. He was admiring a cake made by some kids wearing bright green aprons and matching chefs' hats.

"What an amazing cake!" Poppy Fields exclaimed, as everyone headed over to look.

"Wow!" Kirsty murmured to Rachel. "It really *is* spectacular!"

The enormous cake had been decorated to look like the Rainspell Island seashore. There was an ocean of blue icing swirls, golden sand made of buttercream icing sparkling with edible glitter, and white marshmallow cliffs.

"There's even a model of my lighthouse!" Polly Painterly laughed. "And it's all the right colors, too."

"See the surfers?" said Ben, pointing to a couple of tiny green figures on top of the blue icing waves. "And the boat? This really is a magnificent cake! How did you manage to bake it and decorate it so quickly?" he asked the boys.

"Because we're baking experts, that's why!" one of the kids proclaimed, and the others chuckled.

"This cake will be perfect for the exhibition," Ben told them. "You can take it over to the tent now."

The group of kids proudly carried the cake away. But as they passed the girls, Rachel noticed long green noses poking out from underneath their chefs' hats. She glanced at Kirsty.

"Goblin alert!" Rachel whispered.

The goblins were muttering to each other. Rachel moved a little closer to hear what they were saying.

"We're not sharing this cake," the biggest goblin said. "No way!"

"Let's take it to the beach and eat it ourselves!" a goblin with huge ears suggested. The others cackled with glee.

"Let's follow them, Kirsty," Rachel said urgently. Immediately, the girls went to find Ben.

"We're just going out to get some ideas for decorating our cakes and cookies," Kirsty told him.

"That's fine," Ben agreed.

Rachel and Kirsty quickly took off their aprons and hats, and Roxie hid herself in a pocket of Rachel's shorts. Then they followed the goblins out of the shop. They were just in time to see them heading down the steps to the beach.

"We could keep up with the goblins more easily if we could fly," Rachel suggested. Right on cue, Roxie fluttered out of her pocket.

"Just what I was thinking, girls!"
Roxie cried, her eyes sparkling.

Rachel and Kirsty ducked behind a
wall while Roxie worked her magic. In
no time, the girls became fairy-sized,
with sparkling wings on their shoulders.
Then the three of them zoomed along
the beach until they caught up with the
goblins.

"Stay high above their heads so they don't spot us," Roxie whispered.

From overhead, the girls and Roxie had a better view of the wonderful cake below. Suddenly, Roxie gasped aloud.

"Girls, the goblins definitely used my magic cookie cutter to make shapes for their cake!" she declared with a frown. "See the tiny star on the sail of the boat? And on the flag stuck in the sandcastle?"

"I can see another one, too." Kirsty pointed down at the cake. "It looks like a starfish half-buried in the sand."

Roxie peered down. "That's no starfish," she announced. "That's my magic cookie cutter! Now's our chance to get it back! Any ideas?"

Goblins at Sea

The goblins placed the cake carefully on
top of a flat rock on the beach, then
stood back to admire it.

"I'll eat the lighthouse," the biggest
goblin declared.

"I want that part!" another goblin
grumbled.

"I'll eat the ocean," announced the
goblin with the huge ears.

"That's not fair," the goblin next to him complained. "It's almost half of the cake!"

"So?" the big-eared goblin retorted with a shrug.

All the goblins began arguing loudly over which part of the cake they wanted for themselves.

"Now's our chance, girls," Roxie whispered. "Let's try and dig my magic cookie cutter out of the icing!"

Roxie, Rachel, and Kirsty flew down to the cake, keeping out of the goblins' sight. The goblins were hollering and shrieking at one another, and there was a lot of pushing and shoving going on, too.

Now that they were close to the cake, Rachel could see a faint golden haze of magic around the top of the cookie cutter. "There's just enough sticking out for us to grab onto," Rachel whispered. "If we all pull together—"

But suddenly, Rachel stopped in alarm. A big green goblin hand was sneakily reaching for a chunk of cake—right next to where the three of them were hovering! Roxie quickly pulled the girls to hide in a cave cut in the side of the marshmallow cliffs.

"Stop that!" the big goblin yelled at the cake thief, suddenly spotting what he was up to.

"But I want some cake!" the goblin whined.

As the goblins all continued to argue, Rachel turned to Kirsty and Roxie.

"We're too small to pull out the magic cookie cutter now, but I thought of another way to get it back," Rachel whispered. "Kirsty and I have to be our normal size for it to work, so first we need to escape from this cave!"

Roxie grinned. "The goblins are practically wrestling each other over the cake," she pointed out. "So I think it's safe to leave!"

Roxie and the girls darted out of the cave and back to a nearby wall. The goblins never noticed a thing! A burst of glittery magic from Roxie's wand made Rachel and Kirsty their usual size again.

Rachel explained her plan, and the three of them headed back to the goblins again. Roxie kept out of sight, high above the girls.

"Oh, what a fabulous cake!" Kirsty gasped. All the goblins turned to stare at her, which was just what Rachel was hoping for. It was Kirsty's job to keep the goblins distracted while *she* tried to grab the cookie cutter. "Did you bake it?"

The goblins nodded proudly.

"It looks delicious," Kirsty said eagerly.

"Can I have a little taste?"

The goblins glared at her.

"No way!" screeched the biggest goblin. "This cake is for goblins only!"

"But it's nice to share," Kirsty told him.

"Goblins don't share," the goblin with the huge ears snapped. "Goblins are greedy!"

"*I'm* not greedy," another goblin protested.

"Then give this pesky human girl *your* piece of cake!" said the big-eared goblin.

None of the goblins were looking at the cake, so they didn't see Roxie hovering above it. Meanwhile, Rachel stayed out of sight behind Kirsty and tried to pry the magic cookie cutter out of the buttercream icing. But unfortunately, the goblin who had tried to steal some cake earlier decided to try again while the others were arguing with Kirsty. As he snuck over to the cake, the goblin spotted Rachel and Roxie immediately. He gave an angry cry.

"Get away from our cake!" he yelled.

The other goblins hurried forward, furious, and snatched the cake from under Rachel's nose. They bolted across the beach, carrying the cake above their heads.

"Look!" one of the goblins shouted, pointing at an inflatable boat pulled up on the sand.

The goblins quickly piled into the boat, taking the cake with them. The biggest goblin pushed the boat into the shallow waves, then jumped in himself.

"You can't catch us!" the goblins chanted smugly as they rowed away, leaving Kirsty, Rachel, and Roxie on the beach. "And you're not getting any of our cake, either!"

"What do we do now?" Rachel asked, dismayed.

Kirsty glanced helplessly around the beach for inspiration. Suddenly, she spotted a seagull hopping across the sand. He looked familiar!

"Roxie, that's the seagull who helped us get Josie the Jewelry Fairy's magic ribbon back!" Kirsty explained quickly. "Could you ask him to fly after the goblins and pull the cookie cutter out of the cake with his beak?"

"That's a great idea, Kirsty!" Roxie agreed. She flew over to the seagull and began whispering to him while the girls waited. The seagull cocked his head to one side, listening carefully to what Roxie was saying and squawking a reply. Then,

spreading his enormous white
wings, he launched himself
into the air.

"The seagull
says he remembers
the goblins, and he's
glad to help," Roxie
told the girls. "Let's
hope this works!"

The seagull was already hovering
above the goblins' boat as it bobbed up
and down on the waves. As Roxie and
the girls watched hopefully, the seagull
swooped down, his dark eyes fixed on
the cake.

The goblins shrieked in fear. "Go
away, you horrible bird!" the biggest
goblin yelled, trying to swat the seagull
away.

"He's trying to eat our cake!" another goblin shrieked.

The seagull lunged for the cake as the goblins flailed, trying to frighten him. The seagull tried again, but two of the goblins snatched the cake away just in time. The seagull missed the cake—instead, his beak jabbed into the side of the boat, putting a hole in it!

There was a loud hissing sound as the boat began to deflate.

"Oh, no!" Rachel cried. "We have to do something fast, or the boat will sink . . ."

". . . Taking the cake, Roxie's magic cookie cutter, *and* the goblins with it!" Kirsty added.

Fairy Crafts

The goblins were starting to panic.

"Our boat's sinking!" the biggest goblin shouted. "We'll have to swim for it!"

"Goblins can't swim!" another one yelled. "And, we can't leave the cake behind, anyway!"

"Roxie, we need a boat so we can row out and rescue the goblins," Rachel told the little fairy.

Roxie immediately waved her wand, creating a cloud of fairy magic. When the sparkles faded, another inflatable boat had appeared on the beach. The girls pushed the boat into the shallow water, then jumped in and grabbed the oars. They began to row toward the goblins, with Roxie flying overhead.

"Help!" the biggest goblin shrieked when he spotted the girls. "We're going to drown!"

"No, you're not," Rachel said firmly. "We're going to save you. But first, you need to give Roxie her magic cookie cutter back!"

The biggest goblin looked unsure, but the others turned on him.

"Give it back!" they yelled.

The biggest goblin dug the cookie cutter out of the icing and held it up. With a cry of joy, Roxie swooped down to grab it. At the touch of her tiny fingers, the cookie cutter shrank down to its fairy size.

The girls rowed closer so the goblins could scramble aboard their boat, bringing the cake with them.

"The icing's starting to melt!" the big-eared goblin groaned miserably. "The lighthouse and the surfers have fallen over."

"The cake is ruined!" whined the biggest goblin.

"But I bet it still tastes good," Kirsty reassured them.

Fluttering high above, Roxie used her

magic to divide the cake into slices, and
they each had a piece as the girls rowed
back to shore.

"*Mmm*, it's yummy!" the goblins
declared, their green faces sticky
with icing. They were
still munching away
when the girls
and Roxie left
them on the
beach. Rachel
and Kirsty ran
back to the
bakery, with
Roxie hidden in
the pocket of Rachel's shorts.

The kitchen was filled with delicious
smells when Rachel and Kirsty walked
in.

"Girls, we've been busy while you were away!" Ben declared.

Rachel and Kirsty were thrilled to see that the counters were covered with delicious-looking cakes and cookies. Everything was going smoothly now that

Roxie had her magic cookie cutter back! The girls quickly put on their aprons and chefs' hats, with Roxie taking her place in Kirsty's apron pocket again, and then

they got to work. Rachel made her
lemon drizzle cake, and Kirsty baked a
tray of golden-brown sugar cookies.
Then, thanks to Roxie whispering
helpful instructions, they made a big
batch of cupcakes decorated with beach-
themed shapes—fish, seashells,
lighthouses, and even surfers.

"These are beautiful, girls," Ben said
when they'd finished. "I'll pack them up
and get them ready for the exhibition."

Rachel and Kirsty took a quick look at the other cakes as Ben packed them up.

"This sandcastle cake is amazing!" Rachel marvelled. The cake had towers and turrets, just like a real sandcastle, and it was covered in gold icing with a flag in the top.

"Who made it?" Kirsty asked.

"I did," said one of the helpers, a girl named Jenna. "Ben said I should enter it in the competition."

"Definitely—you should win a prize!" Kirsty told her.

As everyone took off their aprons, Roxie tugged at Kirsty's sleeve. "Are you

coming to Fairyland to see the Magical
Crafts Week exhibition?" she asked.

"We wouldn't miss it for anything!"
Kirsty replied. Calling good-bye to Ben
and the others, the girls hurried outside.
Then Roxie's magic swept them away to
Fairyland!

The crafts exhibition was being held in the Fairyland Palace. The room was packed with fairies, including King Oberon and Queen Titania, who were viewing the display. When Roxie, Rachel, and Kirsty arrived, everyone cheered.

"Girls, you saved our Crafts Week!" declared Kayla the Pottery Fairy.

"What good, true friends you are," said Queen Titania with a sweet smile.

"Thanks to you, we have lots of entries for the competition," King Oberon added. "It's going to be very difficult to choose a winner."

Roxie, Kirsty, and Rachel looked around the exhibition. There were all kinds of beautiful craft projects. The Rainbow Fairies had entered colorful paintings and drawings. The Fashion Fairies had designed and sewn bright, glittering dresses.

As the king and queen discussed the entries they'd seen so far, Rachel and Kirsty saw Cherry the Cake Fairy rush in, followed by the Sugar and Spice Fairies. They were all carrying cakes on gold platters.

"Roxie got her magic cookie cutter back just in time!" Cherry cried. Her spectacular cake was shaped like the Fairyland Palace, complete with four pink towers made of icing.

"Otherwise our baking would have been a total disaster," added Coco the Cupcake Fairy. She held up a plate of cupcakes decorated with miniature fairies that had glittery wings.

Suddenly, a blast of cold air swirled around the room. Seconds later, Jack Frost stormed in, carrying the self-portrait he'd done at Polly Painterly's workshop under his arm. He was also carrying a snowflake-shaped cake, a notebook, a necklace made of icicles, a sketch of his Ice Castle, a clay pot with a white glaze, and a flowing, ice-blue cloak. "I'm entering all the categories!" Jack Frost said with a smug sneer. "My crafts are the best, so I'm going to win first prize!"

And the Winner Is . . .

Just then, King Oberon stepped forward. "The queen and I are happy to announce the winner of Magical Crafts Week," he said. "First prize goes to Cherry the Cake Fairy for her wonderful cake!"

The fairies applauded, but Jack Frost stomped his foot.

"NO!" he roared furiously. "What's the point of doing crafts at all if I don't win the competition?"

"The point is to have fun!" Rachel told him. "Did you enjoy doing your crafts?"

Jack Frost frowned. "Well . . . yes," he admitted reluctantly. "I especially liked painting my self-portrait."

"Trying something new and having fun is the best part," Kirsty said. "That's what really counts. Why don't you hang your self-portrait in your bedroom? Then you can look at it all the time!"

Jack Frost stroked his frozen beard thoughtfully. "Yes, I could do that," he said at last, his icy face breaking into a smile. Then he went off happily to his Ice Castle, taking his crafts with him.

"Girls, thank you a million times over for your help!" Roxie said gratefully, giving them both a hug. "Magical Crafts Week really has been magical because of you. And now," Roxie went on, her eyes twinkling, "you have your own exhibition to attend, so it's probably time for you to go!"

The other fairies gathered around as Roxie prepared to send Rachel and

Kirsty back to Rainspell Island with her magic.

"Congratulations, Cherry," Rachel called. "Good-bye, everybody!"

"Great job, Cherry," Kirsty said. "See you all again soon!"

And with their fairy friends all waving good-bye, the girls were whisked away to Rainspell Island. In the blink of an eye, they found themselves next to the exhibition tent.

"Here come our parents!" Rachel said, spotting her mom and dad and Mr. and Mrs. Tate walking

down the boardwalk. "We're just in time."

"Hello, girls," called Kirsty's dad. "Can't wait to taste all the treats you've been baking!"

"Let's look at the exhibition first," Mrs. Tate said with a smile.

Inside the tent, all the best crafts from the week were on display. Kirsty's painting had been hung on a board with other paintings, and Rachel's notebook had been left open on a table so that everyone could read her story. Jenna's sandcastle cake was there, too, along with pencil sketches of Rainspell Island, silver bracelets and earrings from the jewelry workshop, some glazed clay pots, and sewing projects, including a patchwork quilt of Rainspell Island.

After admiring the displays, the girls and their parents joined the line of people lining up for refreshments.

"Girls, these cupcakes are delicious!" Mr. Tate told them, taking a big bite.

Toward the end of the afternoon, Artie Johnson called for silence in the tent so that she could announce the results of the competition.

"What a difficult but very enjoyable job our judges have had today," Artie said with a smile. "First prize goes to Jenna Barker for her wonderful sandcastle cake!"

Beaming, Jenna hurried forward to accept her prize—a set of craft books—while everyone applauded.

"Now we have a joint second prize to award," Artie continued. "But I know these two girls are great friends, so they won't mind sharing this lovely jewelry-making kit. Second prize goes to Kirsty

Tate for her painting *Rachel Under a Rainbow*, and to Rachel Walker for her story *Rainbow Fairies*!"

Thrilled, the girls went up to receive their prizes.

"I hope all of you have enjoyed Crafts Week," Artie said as the girls rejoined their parents. "I'm sure you've loved trying new crafts. And I've really enjoyed organizing everything, too—it's been a truly magical week!"

Rachel and Kirsty glanced at each other and shared a secret smile. As Artie said, it really *had* been a magical week. And both girls silently hoped that there were many more magical adventures ahead with their fairy friends!

SPECIAL EDITION

Rachel and Kirsty have found all of the
Magical Crafts Fairies' missing magic
objects. Now it's time for them to help

Lila and Myla
the Twins Fairies!

Join their next adventure in this special
sneak peek. . . .

Party Pairs

"This is the house," said Rachel Walker, pointing up at a tall, white townhouse.

A bunch of pink balloons was tied to the gate, and there was another bunch pinned to the front door. Rachel smoothed down her party dress and smiled at her best friend, Kirsty Tate. Kirsty was staying with Rachel during her school vacation.

"It was really nice of your friends to

invite me to their birthday parties," said
Kirsty. "I've never been to two in one
day before!"

Rachel's school friends Jessy and Amy
were twins, and they were having two
separate birthday parties—one for each
of them.

"Jessy and Amy's parents are really
fun," Rachel said as they walked up
to the front door. "They're letting Jessy
have her party this morning, and Amy
have hers this afternoon. The twins like
different music and decorations, and
their mom and dad wanted to make sure
they were both happy!"

She knocked on the door and it was
opened by a pretty girl with long blonde
hair and big blue eyes. She was wearing
a sparkly pink party dress and there was
a pink bow in her hair.

"Happy birthday, Jessy!" said Rachel.

"Thanks," said Jessy with a smile. "This must be Kirsty? Hi!"

"Hi, and happy birthday," said Kirsty.

Jessy invited them in. There were pink balloons pinned into every corner and the guests were dancing to music. A table was piled high with presents wrapped in pink paper.

"Those are the prizes for the party games," Jessy said, seeing Rachel looking at them.

Kirsty peeked into the kitchen and saw a tray full of pink gelatin treats on the dining table.

"Pink's my favorite color," said Jessy with a smile. "Can you tell?"

The girls laughed and gave Jessy their presents. Then another girl came over and gave Rachel a hug.

RAINBOW magic ™

Which Magical Fairies Have You Met?

- ❏ The Rainbow Fairies
- ❏ The Weather Fairies
- ❏ The Jewel Fairies
- ❏ The Pet Fairies
- ❏ The Dance Fairies
- ❏ The Music Fairies
- ❏ The Sports Fairies
- ❏ The Party Fairies
- ❏ The Ocean Fairies
- ❏ The Night Fairies
- ❏ The Magical Animal Fairies
- ❏ The Princess Fairies
- ❏ The Superstar Fairies
- ❏ The Fashion Fairies
- ❏ The Sugar & Spice Fairies
- ❏ The Earth Fairies

■SCHOLASTIC

Find all of your favorite fairy friends at
scholastic.com/rainbowmagic

HIT entertainment

RMFAIRY1

RAINBOW magic ™

SPECIAL EDITION

Which Magical Fairies Have You Met?

3 stories in each one!

- ❑ Joy the Summer Vacation Fairy
- ❑ Holly the Christmas Fairy
- ❑ Kylie the Carnival Fairy
- ❑ Stella the Star Fairy
- ❑ Shannon the Ocean Fairy
- ❑ Trixie the Halloween Fairy
- ❑ Gabriella the Snow Kingdom Fairy
- ❑ Juliet the Valentine Fairy
- ❑ Mia the Bridesmaid Fairy
- ❑ Flora the Dress-Up Fairy
- ❑ Paige the Christmas Play Fairy
- ❑ Emma the Easter Fairy
- ❑ Cara the Camp Fairy
- ❑ Destiny the Rock Star Fairy
- ❑ Belle the Birthday Fairy
- ❑ Olympia the Games Fairy
- ❑ Selena the Sleepover Fairy
- ❑ Cheryl the Christmas Tree Fairy
- ❑ Florence the Friendship Fairy
- ❑ Lindsay the Luck Fairy
- ❑ Brianna the Tooth Fairy
- ❑ Autumn the Falling Leaves Fairy
- ❑ Keira the Movie Star Fairy
- ❑ Addison the April Fool's Day Fairy
- ❑ Bailey the Babysitter Fairy

SCHOLASTIC

Find all of your favorite fairy friends at
scholastic.com/rainbowmagic

HIT entertainment

RMSPECIAL13

RAINBOW magic™

These activities are magical!
Play dress-up, send friendship notes,
and much more!

SCHOLASTIC
www.scholastic.com
www.rainbowmagiconline.com

RMACTIV